Peanut Butter and Jelly

#5 NOT STARRING JILLY!

Look for these and other books
in the PEANUT BUTTER
AND JELLY series:

#5 NOT STARRING JILLY!

Dorothy Haas

Illustrated by Jeffrey Lindberg

A
LITTLE APPLE
PAPERBACK

SCHOLASTIC INC.
New York Toronto London Auckland Sydney

ISBN 0-590-42392-4

12 11 10 9 8 7 6 5 4 3 2 1   9/8 0 1 2 3 4/9

Printed in the U.S.A.   28

First Scholastic printing, October 1989

#5 NOT STARRING JILLY!

CHAPTER
1

"This list looks almost like a recipe," said Polly Butterman, better known to her friends as Peanut. "It says: Two gnomes, two girls, two — "

"Princes," read Jilly, peeking over her shoulder at the list. "Two bears. Everything comes in twos."

"There's only one mother," said Peanut. "You know, it's kind of funny that there's always a mother in fairy tales but hardly ever a father."

"Unless he's a king," said Jilly. "And then mostly he's a mean one."

"Watch what you say about fathers." Mr. Matthews, Jilly's father, spoke without looking up from his drawing board. The girls were in his studio at the top of the Matthews's house having an after-school snack at the low, round table under the eaves. "Us old dads" — he added a line to his drawing — "get hurt feelings very easily."

"Oh, Daddy!" said Jilly. "You know what I mean. In fairy tales, kings always give their daughter's hand in marriage to some old frog."

"Who always turns out to be a prince," Mr. Matthews reminded her. "What else have you got for your recipe?"

"Gold. There's got to be gold in it."

Jilly was thoughtful. "You know," she said, "we don't really have to make up a story."

"We do, too," Peanut insisted. "That's what Miss Kraft said — do something creative with these things in it. That means a story."

2

"Well, see," said Jilly, "the parts I like best about stories are people talking."

"Me, too." Peanut took a bite out of her graham cracker, a perfect half-circle bite. "The parts I don't like so much are the long ones that tell how the little cottage in the woods looked with the birds tweeting around it. Sometimes I skip those parts."

"So what I mean is," said Jilly, "why don't we make up a fairy tale that's like a play — just talking."

Peanut's face lit up. "What a great idea! We can just talk it at each other and write down what we say."

Jilly grinned. "Easy," she said.

"Nothing to it," Peanut agreed.

"Don't be too sure about that," said Mr. Matthews, holding up the drawing of a food blender he was working on and squinting at it. "That's what Michelangelo said when he started painting the ceiling of the Sistine Chapel — easy . . . I can do it lying down. He got a terrible crick in his neck."

Peanut and Jilly ignored him.

"We can start right now," said Jilly. "Let's be the girls. My name is . . . is . . . Alexandra."

"I'll be Stephanie," said Peanut. "Suppose we're gathering wood in the forest for our poor old mother who — "

A ruckus came from the stairwell.

There was a delighted screech from Jackie, Jilly's little brother.

"Hang on tight," Jerry, her older brother, cautioned.

"What's going on down there?" called Mr. Matthews.

"A piggyback ride," Jackie shouted. "I'm coming up there on my horse. I mean my pig."

"Watch it, Jerry," Mr. Matthews called. "He's too heavy for you to carry."

There was a thumping on the stairs and Jerry staggered into view. He was bent over double, with Jackie on his back. He leaned to one side and Jackie slid off.

"Someday I'm going to be as strong as you, Jerry," Jackie said admiringly.

"Nothing to it," said Jerry. But his face was red and he was breathing hard.

"I'd rather you didn't practice weight lifting on the stairway," said Mr. Matthews. "Somebody's going to fall — and it's a long way down to the bottom of those stairs."

"If you'd get me some weights," said Jerry, "I wouldn't have to practice on Jackie."

"I don't mind," said Jackie. "I'll help you get muscles. Daddy," he went on, "you can save money if you get Jerry some weights because I can use 'em when he outgrows them." He looked around at everybody, pleased at the way he had figured that out.

Trying not to look too proud, Jerry got milk out of the refrigerator and poured it into glasses for himself and Jackie.

"We'll see," said Mr. Matthews. "We'll see."

"What'cha doing?" asked Jackie, coming to the table for an apple, eyeing the sheet of paper Peanut still held.

"We're going to write a play," said Peanut.

"I'll help you." Jackie was all seriousness.

"I know a lot about playing. I go to play camp in summer."

Jilly couldn't help laughing. "Not that kind of play, Jack-O. This is like a story with real people in it."

"Like TV?" asked Jackie.

"Live people," said Peanut. "Like they are on a stage and they act like they're somebody else."

"Little kid stuff," snorted Jerry, spraying the air with crumbs.

"It is *not* little kid stuff!" Jilly said hotly. "Little kids can't write a story or a play."

"Can, too," said Jackie. "I told Mom a story and she wrote it all down just the way I said it."

"Make it about some really strong guys," suggested Jerry. "Wrestlers."

"Ugh," said Jilly. "What's fun about wrestlers?"

"Anyway," said Peanut, "we've got to use the things on this list from Miss Kraft."

Jilly sighed deeply. Why was it that when

Jerry came into a room everything interesting stopped? "Let's go down to my room," she said to Peanut. "We can work there without interruptions from silly people."

"Silly, shmilly." Jerry grinned maddeningly. "You're really dumb."

"Quiet, you two," ordered Mr. Matthews. "At times I think you're aliens from different planets. Try to get along."

Jilly drained her milk and picked out an apple. "Let's go."

Peanut took another graham cracker. She hadn't had graham crackers in a long time. She had forgotten how good they were.

They went downstairs and into Jilly's bedroom on the second floor of the big, old house. Peanut stopped just inside the door, looking at the floor, her hands lifted in surprise. "Oh, oh, Alexandra! Look at the nice piece of dry wood on the floor — I mean ground. It will make a fine fire."

"Why, thank you, dear Stephanie, for pointing it out to me." Jilly pretended to pick up something. "I almost stumbled over it."

8

They worked on their play until it was time for Peanut to go home for dinner. That evening they talked on the phone, each taking a part in their play, until Mrs. Butterman made Peanut hang up.

Writing a play was the best thing they had done in weeks and weeks.

CHAPTER 2

▼■▼■▼■▼■▼■▼■▼■▼■▼■▼■▼

"Well, yes, Nathan, I did say to be creative," said Miss Kraft. "And you may make up a board game with the characters, if you like. But I really meant for you to write something. That's what this assignment is all about."

"Aw, heck," said Nate. "I even started making the board."

Miss Kraft smiled at him. "Please me, Nate. Do some writing for me."

Nate wiggled around in his seat. "Oh, all right," he said at last.

"I know I'm going to like what you do," said Miss Kraft.

Nate brightened and began writing.

"Miss Kraft?" Peanut spoke for herself and Jilly. "Instead of writing a story, we're making up a play together. Is that okay?"

"What an interesting idea," said Miss Kraft. Then she added, "But you heard what I just told Nate. The purpose of this project is to write. Use your best writing skills — all the things we've been talking about this last month."

Peanut had another question. "The people on the list — do we have to use them all?"

"Well. . . . " Miss Kraft was thoughtful. "Everybody else is using the complete list. Is it fair if you don't?"

Peanut and Jilly looked at each other and agreed without saying a word. That wouldn't be fair. So they would use all the characters. "Can we add someone not on the list?" asked Jilly.

"What Jilly means," Peanut hastily added,

"is we've got a great idea for a dragon. Can we use him?"

"Let's talk about this. Come to my desk," said Miss Kraft. She looked around the room. "Those of you in the writing group, get to work on your stories. Pilgrims" — Pilgrims were the special reading group — "suppose you gather in the reading corner. Kevin, see that everyone has a book. I'll be with you in a minute. Now, girls" — she turned to Peanut and Jilly, who had come to her desk — "fill me in on what you're up to."

So they told her about liking the talking parts of books.

"That's called dialogue," said Miss Kraft.

And about thinking it would be fun to write a play together.

"We'll make it as long as two stories put together," promised Jilly.

And they told about how they were talking the parts.

"But we've really got to have a dragon," said Peanut.

"All right," said Miss Kraft. "I'll tell every-

one they may add characters to their stories if they wish. Now, how many acts will you have?"

"Acts?" asked Jilly.

"Acts are like the chapters in a book," explained Miss Kraft. "They are the different parts of the story."

Jilly thought she understood. "Like in TV, the story makes you wonder about something and then it stops for a commercial."

"Something like that," said Miss Kraft. "There are other things you will want to know. Talk to me after school this afternoon. Now the two of you settle down in a corner. Keep your voices low. Don't disturb the others."

She went to the reading corner, and Peanut and Jilly sat on the floor near the supply cabinets, their notebooks on their knees, whispering, writing.

"Hee hee," Peanut chuckled wickedly, writing as she spoke. "Us gnomes are going to fix that king. He thinks nobody knows where he keeps his gold."

"We'll put an enchantment on him and on

the gold, too," Jilly said in a hoarse gnome voice. "We'll turn him into a dragon and the gold into . . . into . . . wilted flowers." She wrote furiously.

"And then we'll have all the gold in the world," Peanut chortled. "All. All. All."

"Baaaa-lammmmmm!" murmured Jilly. "That's how an enchantment sounds," she explained. "Baaaa-lammmmm!"

"Sounds more like a sheep to me," said Peanut.

"So if you know what an enchantment sounds like, *you* say the word."

"Vaaa-roooom!"

"That's not an enchantment — it's a fast car!"

"Oh, all right. Baaaa-lammmmm!"

"We can change it later if we think of a better word."

Writing a play, it became clear, was harder than either of them thought it would be. They worked on it for days and days and days. Well, actually, the days were all of that week and part of the next. Some of the time they worked in class. The rest of the time they worked on it after school. And they talked on the phone as much as their mothers would allow.

"You know," said Peanut, "Stephanie is exactly like me. She laughs all the time. She's noisy. She isn't afraid of anything or anybody."

"Alexandra is like me, I guess," said Jilly. "Sort of quiet. Kind of" — she said the awful word — "shy." She hated it when people called her shy. It made her more shy! But she could talk about it to Peanut. She could talk about *anything* to Peanut. "You know," she said, "when I feel that way I make myself do whatever it is I have to do."

Peanut thought about that. Being scared and not giving in to it took a special kind of courage. "You're a really brave person," she said.

"That's what my dad says," said Jilly. "It doesn't always help, though."

"Do you ever wonder why you're shy?" Peanut asked curiously.

"Do you ever wonder why you're not?" Jilly said pertly.

16

What a question! Of course Peanut never wondered why she wasn't shy. "My mom says I'm outgoing," she said. "I guess I was born that way."

"I guess I was born sort of in-going," said Jilly.

"Since we're making up a story and talking it," said Peanut, "I guess Stephanie and Alexandra are going to be like us."

"Is everybody in the story like us, then?" wondered Jilly. "The princes? King William the Wonderful? The poor old mother?"

Peanut jumped on the idea. "The gnomes! Hey! Neither of them is shy."

"They're horrible," said Jilly. "We aren't mean and horrible."

"I guess we're just pretending with them," said Peanut. "You can be anything you want when you pretend."

"Like pretending to be a king turned into a dragon," said Jilly.

How did a dragon act? Kind like the king he really was? Or mean the way dragons are said to be? They decided to let Dragon Hotbreath have a kindly heart, even though he breathed fire. There still was a problem with him and the story, though.

"Which of us is he going to fall in love with when he turns into King William the Wonderful?"

"Stephanie!"

"Alexandra!"

"But then the ending won't be happy ever after for everybody. One of the princesses won't have anybody. And fairy tales are supposed to have happy-ever-after endings for everybody."

"Well, would he fall in love with their mother?"

"Listen, I've got an idea! The bears — we haven't used them yet — are really the king's sons. They are enchanted, too."

"They can fall in love with Alexandra and Stephanie."

"What'll we call the princes? They have to have royal-sounding names."

"How about Bryan? I like that name."

"And Ryan! Bryan and Ryan!"

And so several problems were solved. But a

problem solved always seemed to lead to another one, like what to do about the gold-turned-into-wilted-flowers. And how to lift the enchantment from Dragon Hotbreath.

"Maybe someone does something kind. Like the dragon can do a kind deed. It's surprising when a dragon is kind."

"The kindest thing you can do for wilted flowers is give them water."

"And then they straighten up and look fresh."

"And turn back into gold?"

"Gold flowers?"

"How pretty!"

The parts of the story worked out, bit by bit. At last they cut up the talk they had written down and pasted the pieces onto pages. They ended up with a lot of pages stuck full of flaps and bits of paper. They had thirteen acts.

"Don't you think thirteen is a lot?" asked Miss Kraft when she read their play.

Thirteen did seem like a lot when she said that.

"All right," she said. "You are in over your

19

heads. I'll help you consolidate the action."

Con-sol-i-date. . . . Peanut and Jilly exchanged puzzled looks.

"That means squeeze it together," said Miss Kraft. "You can have some of the action in the woods. And some in front of the cottage. Instead of having the girls meet the dragon on a cliff, why not have him come to the cottage? I think that will work. And. . . ."

They ended up with just six acts. The last act was the wedding of King William the Wonderful and the girls' mother.

"Stephanie and Alexandra will be bridesmaids," said Peanut.

"They will carry bouquets of golden flowers," said Jilly.

"The princes will wear crowns of golden flowers," said Peanut.

Yes, the play had turned into a very satisfactory story.

CHAPTER
3

■▼■▼■▼■▼■▼■▼■▼■▼■▼■▼■

"All right," Peanut's big sister, Ceci, sighed. "The two of you have worn me down. I'll put your play into my computer. Let's see what you've got."

Peanut withdrew her hand from behind her back and offered a bunch of pages. Bits and pieces of paper stuck up all over it.

Ceci slapped her forehead with the palm of her hand. "What a mess!"

"There's more," said Peanut. She dug her elbow into Jilly's ribs, and Jilly passed along the rest of the play.

Ceci flipped through the messy pages. "You mean to tell me your teacher read this?"

"Miss Kraft is really nice," said Jilly.

"She doesn't think our writing is so terrible," said Peanut.

"She helped us scrunch it together," said Jilly.

"Scrunch?" asked Ceci.

"Well, see, we had thirteen acts," explained Peanut. "And — "

"You had — thir-*teen*?" Ceci exploded with laughter.

"I don't see what's funny," Peanut said with great dignity. "Miss Kraft didn't laugh. She just helped us fix it so that now we've just got six acts."

Ceci's mouth quirked upward at the corners. "Oh, that's much better. So okay, I'll type it. But you've got to stay right here in this room to help me with the words I can't figure out."

She settled down at her computer and stacked the pasted-up pages next to her keyboard.

"I'll get us some soda," said Peanut. "Do you want a Coke?"

"The diet kind," murmured Ceci, reading.

"Come on," Peanut said to Jilly. "You can help me carry it."

"Your sister is really nice," Jilly said as they got soda out of the refrigerator. "I wish I had a sister. Old Jerry wouldn't type anything for me, even if he knew how to. Sisters are nicer than brothers."

"Maggie's my sister, too, and *she* wouldn't help me," said Peanut. "Anyway," she added as they left the kitchen, "you've got Jackie. He's the most wonderful little boy I've ever met."

Jilly agreed. Jackie was the sweetest little kid around. And he *was* a brother.

Peanut paused to poke around in the drawer of the telephone stand at the foot of the stairs. She held up a box of pick-up sticks. "Let's play while we wait."

They went back upstairs, settled on the floor beside Ceci's four-poster bed, and Peanut dumped the sticks out of their box. "You first," she said. "You pick up as many as you can without moving any of the others."

Jilly picked up the five easiest ones. But the stack moved when she tried for the sixth.

"My turn, my turn," crowed Peanut.

"Here — what does this say?" asked Ceci.

Peanut got up to look. "Porridge," she said, reading over Ceci's shoulder. " 'Alas, the porridge is gone.' Isn't it funny how they always call cereal *porridge* in fairy tales?"

"And they say *alas* a lot," Jilly added, from the floor.

"Okay," said Ceci, starting to type again. "Back to your game."

Carefully, oh so carefully, Peanut pulled three sticks out of the jumble. She used to be pretty good at this game. But maybe she had lost her touch. The stack of sticks moved the next time she tried.

Ceci stopped typing and leaned back in her chair, laughing. "Hotbreath? You named your dragon Hotbreath?"

Peanut and Jilly looked at each other. What was funny about Hotbreath?

"He breathes fire," said Peanut. "That's a good name for a dragon."

"Should we change his name?" asked Jilly. It would be very hard to find another name as good as Hotbreath.

Ceci stopped laughing. "Absolutely not," she said, her breath catching, her cheeks pink. "I love it!"

Ceci typed and Peanut and Jilly played at pick-up sticks, interrupting themselves whenever Ceci needed help with a word.

"That's *thither* — 'Go thither, you silly goose.' One of the gnomes says that to Alexandra."

" 'Forsooth, Dragon, you cannot free yourself from our enchantment.' The other gnome says that."

"Frock."

"Fetch."

"Alack."

All the old-fashioned fairy-tale words were there.

Peanut settled back on her heels. "This game isn't as much fun as it used to be. I wonder why."

"Because you're growing up," said Ceci, without looking up from her typing. "You like harder things."

When the pages started coming out of the printer, Peanut and Jilly gave up on pick-up sticks and read the pages excitedly. They looked wonderful. Each speaker's name was at the left followed by whatever that speaker said.

"I'll bet Miss Kraft is really going to like this," Peanut said, stroking the pages.

"Let's hope so," said Ceci, "seeing as how I've given up my Sunday afternoon to type it. There. The end." She eyed them. "There's a copy here for each of you and one for your teacher. And now" — she grinned — "suppose, forsooth, you two go thither so I can work on my history. We're having a test this week."

Going downstairs, hugging their copies of the play, Peanut and Jilly felt pleased and proud of what they had done with the list Miss

Kraft had given them. It was just the best play. And it looked really grown-up, all typed and everything.

"I can hardly wait for tomorrow," said Jilly.

Peanut had a horrible thought. "We all had the same things to put into our stories. Do you suppose our stories will be exactly alike?"

Tomorrow. They would find out tomorrow when everybody shared their stories.

Courtney's story was about two girls who helped their old mother bake tarts to sell at a fair. Two bears bought them, and so did a unicorn, the extra character she had added. The story was all in verse. "I think I can make it better," she said. "I rhymed tart and cart and that's kind of corny."

But everyone thought the story was great just as it was. Nobody could write poetry the way Courtney did.

Nate's story was about two magician bears who cast spells on people who didn't give them their gold. He had finished his board game as well.

"Look," he said, "the playing pieces have bears and gnomes on them. Want to play after school?" he asked Elena.

"But you know all the rules. You'll win," said Elena.

"That's not the way it works," said Nate. "Play and find out."

Emmy and Erin had worked on their story together and printed it in a book with pictures. It was about two girls who lived in an ice castle. Emmy had to read the story alone, though. Erin wasn't in school. She had chicken pox.

David's story was about a prince who solved mysteries. He wore disguises. Sometimes he was a gnome, sometimes a bear. He had made his story into a comic book. The talk was all in balloons above the characters' heads.

"David's story is all talk, too," Peanut whispered as they went to the front of the room.

"And all the stories are different," said Jilly. "They aren't one bit alike. I wonder how that happens."

They read their play, taking all the parts.

It was so much fun that Jilly forgot about feeling strange and shy, reading in front of everybody. She was the gentle mother. She was one of the handsome princes. She outdid herself as a — hee-hee-hee — mean old gnome.

"Girl stuff," Ollie muttered when Stephanie and Alexandra wept over the field of wilted flowers.

Carrie clasped her hands and sighed happily when the king married the girls' mother and Stephanie and Alexandra were bridesmaids.

Peanut and Jilly went back to their desks feeling as though they had been climbing a high mountain and were standing on the very tip-top.

Miss Kraft got up from her desk. "You all did beautifully," she said. "I am very proud of you!"

Everyone grinned.

"These are too good to keep to ourselves," Miss Kraft continued. "We are going to share them with the rest of the school. I'll arrange with Mrs. Harris to put them on display in the Learning Center so that everybody at

Alcott School can see and enjoy them."

Everyone looked around at each other, pleased and proud of what they had done.

Miss Kraft continued. "I have something else in mind. A play isn't really finished until it's performed."

Peanut and Jilly turned to each other, their eyes round.

"I'm going to ask my friend Miss Maya Schultz if she would like to direct our play," said Miss Kraft. "Miss Schultz is a very talented actress."

They were going to *do* the play? With actors and costumes and everything?

Jilly sat at her desk, unmoving. She had forgotten, with all the fun of writing the play, that plays are meant to be acted. That people, a whole lot of people — an audience — watched. Oh!

CHAPTER
4

Miss Maya Schultz came to the room before the last bell rang the next afternoon. She was very glamorous. Her long dark hair, tied with a floaty pink scarf high on her head, fell almost to her waist. Hoop earrings dangled to her shoulders. Her eyes were outlined with lots of makeup.

"Miss Schultz and I were in college together," said Miss Kraft. "She is home visiting for a few weeks before she goes into another play."

Miss Schultz flashed a dazzling smile, looking around, meeting everyone's eyes. "We're going to have lots of fun," she said. "This afternoon we'll have tryouts. Each of you will read some of the lines from the play."

"All of you who want to be in the play raise your hands," said Miss Kraft.

Hands went up, waving, all around the room.

Jilly sat at her desk, frozen. Being in the play would mean standing up and talking in front of everyone. Not just the kids in class, but the whole school. The thought made her middle twitch. Butterflies began playing tag in her stomach.

The last bell rang. Nobody paid any attention. Lifting her voice, Miss Schultz talked right through the whooping and hollering and locker-door slamming in the hall. "I have read the play," she said, "and I want to congratulate the authors on their work. Jillian?" Her eyes swept the room. "Polly?"

Peanut and Jilly raised their hands.

Miss Schultz flashed her beautiful smile. "Good work. Now," she went on, "we will need three girls for the parts of Alexandra and

33

Stephanie and the mother. We will need three boys for the king and the princes after they are freed of their enchantments. We will also need two gnomes and two bears, but they can be either girls or boys, and — "

"Hey!" Ollie interrupted. "Gnomes are little old men."

"Not on stage," said Miss Schultz. "Behind their long white beards, they can be girls or boys."

Elvis nearly fell out of his seat laughing. "I want to see Jilly in a long white beard," he gasped.

Jilly shrank inside herself.

"Can I be the dragon?" asked Ollie. "A girl can't be a dragon. It takes a tough guy like me. I can roar like anything."

"Let me go on," said Miss Schultz. "I have just mentioned the speaking parts. There will be nonspeaking parts, too, so that everyone can be on stage. We will need squirrels, rabbits, and beavers.

"To begin, I will ask each of you to read a few lines. That will tell me which of you have

voices that will carry through a big place like your gym. It will tell me which of you best match the parts, too," she added. "Girls first. Come to the front of the room."

The girls all rushed to be first. All but Jilly.

Jilly sat at her desk, rubbing at a scratch in the wood. What should she do? Should she just get up and go home? Because she couldn't — she just could *not* — stand up and talk while the whole school stared at her.

Suddenly she felt an arm around her shoulders.

"Jilly?" Miss Kraft spoke in a low voice. "Don't you want to be in your play?"

All Jilly could do was shake her head.

"You'd have lots of fun," said Miss Kraft. "You'd see how your story ideas come to life with real people."

Panic washed over Jilly. "You won't make me, will you? Please don't make me be in the play."

"Of course I won't!" Miss Kraft gave her a comforting squeeze. "I just don't want you to miss out on the fun. But there are lots of jobs with a play that don't require acting." She lifted her voice and spoke across the room to Miss Schultz. "We have our stage manager here," she said. "And our prompter. Jilly certainly must know all the lines for all the parts."

"Wonderful!" said Miss Schultz. "Those are hard jobs to fill." She smiled at Jilly. "I'm so glad you will do them."

Miss Kraft gave Jilly a little hug. "There. It's all fixed."

Jilly let out a sigh. She felt as though a ton of bricks had just slid off her shoulders.

"You can get started right away," said Miss Schultz. "Come stand beside me and see how being a prompter and stage manager will feel."

Peanut grabbed Jilly's arm as she passed the girls' group. "You can't not be in our play," she whispered. "It was all your idea. And you *are* Alexandra!" She looked surprised and hurt.

"I can't," whispered Jilly. "I would just die."

Miss Kraft came up behind them. "There

are many ways of being in a play, Polly. What Jilly is doing will be just as satisfying as any of the speaking parts."

Peanut shook her head. Sometimes she didn't understand Jilly. Not at all.

They took turns reading the parts. Then they stood next to each other so that Miss Schultz could see who was tall and who was short.

The boys did the same thing. And then everybody hunkered down to see who could act like rabbits and squirrels and beavers.

"I want to thank you all," Miss Schultz said at last. "I'll be thinking about this tonight. Tomorrow, Miss Kraft will tell you who will play the different parts."

Peanut waited until they got out into the hall and were pulling on their jackets before she exploded. "How can you! How can you not be in our play? You'll miss all the fun!"

"Ha! That's what you say," said Jilly.

"Being in a play is like playing make-believe when you were little," said Peanut.

Jilly's mind could not be changed.

"It won't be any fun without you," wailed Peanut.

"But I'll be right there," said Jilly. "You heard what Miss Kraft said. I'll be the prompter and the stage manager." She thought for a minute. "I wonder what a stage manager does," she said.

"I guess Miss Schultz will tell you," said Peanut. Suddenly she thought of tomorrow. "I can hardly wait to find out who gets to play what parts." A terrible idea suddenly drove all thoughts of Jilly's fears out of Peanut's mind. "What if — what if I don't get to be Stephanie!"

Oh, that couldn't be! Or — could it?

CHAPTER
5

■▼■▼■▼■▼■▼■▼■▼■▼■▼■

Peanut wasn't the only person wondering. Everybody got to school early the next morning. They were hanging around the door when Miss Kraft arrived and followed her to their room.

"Did you decide who gets to be the bears?"

"Who's going to be Alexandra? And Stephanie?"

"What about the gnomes?"

"Who's gonna get to be the dragon?" Ollie's voice drowned out all the others.

"Let me just put my books on my desk,"

pleaded Miss Kraft. "We'll talk in a minute."

Peanut hung back. She was almost afraid to find out who was going to play the part of Stephanie.

Jilly patted her arm. "You don't have to worry. Miss Kraft would never *not* have you in your own play."

They trailed into the room and Peanut went straight to her seat, not joining the crowd at Miss Kraft's desk.

Jilly followed her. "Move over," she whispered. She wasn't going to let Peanut have bad news — if it was bad news — sitting all by herself.

Peanut wriggled onto half the seat and Jilly took the other half. It was a tight fit.

Miss Kraft dug a sheet of paper out of her briefcase. "Miss Schultz and I gave a lot of thought to the play last night," she said. "There are many reasons, as she explained, for filling the parts as we finally did."

Ollie groaned loudly. "Aw, come on," he begged. "Tell us. I can't stand all this waiting around."

"Try to be a little patient, Oliver," Miss Kraft said mildly. "I'll get to your name in a moment."

"That means I got a part!" said Ollie. "You've got my name on your list. All *right!*" He looked around and let out an earsplitting roar.

Miss Kraft winced.

Ollie grinned. "That's what dragons do," he explained.

"Okay, here we go," said Miss Kraft. "Erin?" She looked up from her list. Erin wasn't there. "Is she still sick? Oh, I'm sure she'll be well in time to be a rabbit, along with Rachel. April, Beth, and Todd — you will be squirrels. Andy, Luke — " She looked around. Luke wasn't there. "Don't tell me Luke is sick, too. He — along with Andy and Ben — will be beavers."

"Those are the shortest kids," Jilly murmured in Peanut's ear.

"Now getting on with it: Polly, you will play Stephanie."

Peanut felt as though a giant sun had turned its brightness onto her.

Jilly hugged her.

42

"Carrie will play Alexandra," continued Miss Kraft.

"That's supposed to be you!" muttered Peanut, giving Jilly an accusing look.

"I only wanted to write a story," Jilly whispered, "not act in one."

"Courtney will be the mother," Miss Kraft went on.

"That's because she's tallest," Jilly whispered.

"Aw, come on," begged Ollie. "Who's gonna be the dragon?"

"I'll put your mind at rest, Oliver," said Miss Kraft. "We did decide you'd be a perfect dragon."

"Way to go!" Ollie let out another roar. "Hey — can I take fire-breathing lessons?"

Miss Kraft ignored him. Elena and Allison were going to be the gnomes. David would be King William. Elvis and Emmy were to be the bears. Nate and Jason would play the two princes after they were set free from the enchantment. Kevin would be a page.

"Like in a book?" he asked, puzzled.

"You," Miss Kraft explained, "will step out

onto the stage at the beginning of each act and hold up big cards that say act one, act two, and so on."

"I think I can do that," Kevin said seriously, "if someone tells me when."

"The stage manager will see that you do it at the right time," said Miss Kraft.

Jilly began to get an idea of what a stage manager does.

"All right now, people." Miss Kraft became serious. "The play is going to be fun. But we've got to keep up with our work, too. If we fall behind, our principal will say that having a play is a bad idea and that will be the end of that."

Everyone groaned.

"We don't want Mr. Granger to decide anything like that and so you must promise me that when we work, we'll work with no fooling around. Can you agree to that?"

"Promise." "Promise." "Promise." The word echoed around the room.

"Maybe we can even work fast," said Elena, "so that we'll have more time for the play."

"That remains to be seen," said Miss Kraft.

In the days and weeks that followed, Miss Kraft had the best behaved, the most orderly, the quietest class in Alcott School. They even seemed to learn faster, as Elena had thought they might. And they did it all in addition to practicing for the play, which they did after school and on Saturdays. Nobody minded spending the extra time at school.

For the first practice, they just stayed in their room, reading the play aloud, with everybody taking their parts. But things got more exciting the day Miss Schultz took them to the gym and they stood on the stage, reading their lines.

Miss Schultz sat at the back of the gym, calling directions. "Send your voice right back here to me, Courtney. Everybody in the gym must be able to hear you." "Read that line again, Gnome. Can you sound more gruff?"

The people who weren't reading began to fidget. The rabbits and squirrels and beavers went bonkers, hopping around the stage. When

those with speaking lines told them to stop, they said they were practicing, too.

Things got better when Miss Marsh, the phys ed teacher, came for the forest creatures. "Everybody take note," she called. "You see children leaving with me. In a week or two" — she leaned forward, her eyes round, and spoke in a hushed voice — "rabbits and squirrels and beavers will return to you. Come on, creatures," she said to her charges, "let's go turn into somebody else."

Things were more organized after the forest creatures left. The gym got even quieter when Miss Kraft called the boys together and said she had decided she would practice separately with them back in the classroom.

"But the dragon talks to the mother," said Jilly, watching them leave. "How can we really practice without him?"

"We will send for the boys as they're needed," said Miss Schultz. "Now let's get on with the blocking."

Blocking?

"That means I plan how everyone moves

around on the stage. I'll want you to take notes, Jillian, to help me remember what I decide."

She clapped her hands.

"Stephanie! Alexandra!" she called. "Let's do the first act. You enter from stage left, looking for wood. Go right to the center of the stage."

"Come in. Left," Jilly wrote next to their names on her copy of the play. "Go to center." She was acting like a real stage manager.

CHAPTER 6

There had never been so much for everybody to talk about. On the way to school. Going home afterward. At recess, during lunch, during gym class, on the phone in the evening. And, of course, during play practice.

"Miss Maya" — that's what Miss Schultz had told them to call her — "is the most glamorous lady I ever met."

"Jilly, you're really lucky to be next to her all the time."

"Did you know we'll get to wear makeup for the play? Lipstick and blusher and eyeshadow."

"Jilly, don't you wish you were in the play instead of stage manager? Then you could wear lipstick, too."

"Erin, it's a good thing you got well in time to practice for the play. It takes a lot of practice to learn how to be a rabbit."

"Did you hear that some of the kids in Mr. Moore's class have chicken pox, too? I heard Miss Kraft say it's going around."

"How soon will Mr. Fortunato finish making the scenery?"

"Won't it be fun when we get to practice with the cottage and the trees and the cave?"

"And the flowers. How is Mr. Fortunato going to make them stand up straight and turn into gold after Dragon Hotbreath waters them?"

"Ollie says he's going to figure out some way to breathe fire and wipe out the gnomes."

"Oh, he can't! Miss Maya would never let him!"

"Miss Kraft told my mother if the play goes well at assembly, we might put it on later for the mothers and fathers."

"My mom would like that. She's been making my costume and says she wants to see me in it."

Yes, there was lots to talk about, lots to think about, during the weeks they practiced the play.

When they began to practice with parts of their costumes, everybody started to feel as though they really were their characters.

Erin and Rachel wore long rabbit ears held onto their heads with elastic, and the beavers wore big front teeth. Ollie had to learn to move around with his dragon tail behind him, even though he didn't have the rest of his costume. And Peanut wore a long skirt, just to get the feeling.

Peanut began to feel as though she really were Stephanie, the pretty sister who might one day marry Prince Ryan and become Princess Stephanie. She walked with her head held high, practically glowing with beauty. Oh, she most definitely felt beautiful! And kind, too — that's how a princess is supposed to feel.

One day at practice, caught up in her part,

she leaned down graciously and patted rabbits Erin and Rachel on the head. They looked up at her from their knees, their paws under their chins, and twitched their noses at her.

But when she tried to be royally kind and pet beavers Luke and Andy, that was something else again.

"Keep your mitts off my head," growled Luke, "or I'll sink my teeth into your leg."

"Yeah," muttered Andy. "Remember, these teeth cut down trees. How'd you like your leg to turn into a log for a dam?"

Peanut was careful after that to be kindly only to the rabbits and girl squirrels. But she still felt beautiful.

Jilly didn't stand next to Miss Maya anymore. Miss Maya sat at the back of the gym, calling directions. Jilly stood offstage, at the side, telling the actors when to go onstage and prompting them when they forgot their lines. Elvis was terrible about not remembering his lines.

"Elvis," Miss Maya said the day before dress rehearsal, "if you don't have your lines down

pat, every single one, tomorrow, I'm going to remove you from your part."

Elvis, who had been fooling around with Nate, hanging on a rope backstage, suddenly looked serious. "But you can't! Everybody's used up. I mean, there aren't any guys left."

"Try me," Miss Maya said airily. "I'll find somebody. Kevin would love to be a bear, I'm sure."

Kevin, who was standing beside Jilly, was frightened. "I can't," he moaned. "I don't know how to say all those things."

"Shhhh," Jilly said soothingly. "You don't have to worry, Kev. Miss Maya is just scaring Elvis so he'll really work on his part tonight."

"All right now, everyone," Miss Maya said. "Go home tonight and think about your parts. Run through your lines. Think about where you're supposed to be, and when.

"Bring your costumes to school in the morning. Dress rehearsal will start at three-thirty sharp. When school lets out, Miss Marsh will be waiting to help you" — she looked around at the girls — "put on your costumes in the girls' lavatory — "

"Aaarghhhh," groaned the boys who hadn't been listening carefully. "We're not going into the girls' lavatory."

"Let me finish," said Miss Maya. "Mr. Fortunato will help you boys with your costumes in the boys' lavatory. When you're dressed, you will all go back to your room where Miss Kraft will put on your makeup."

"Makeup!" yelled the boys. "No way!"

"You need it so people in the audience can see your faces clearly," Miss Maya said calmly. "All actors, even the men, wear makeup."

"I'm not wearing any dumb girls' makeup," Ollie said loudly.

"Fortunately you won't need to," said Miss Maya. "Your dragon head will cover your face completely."

"It's a good head," said Ollie. "But I sure wish I could breathe fire."

Miss Maya ignored him. "I'd like our dress rehearsal to go smoothly. But I'm sure it won't be perfect. Funny things happen at dress rehearsals, but that's why we have them — so that all the bugs can be worked out before the real performance."

She looked around at everybody. They were all very serious. Her voice grew soft. "You know," she said, "I think this is the nicest cast I've ever worked with." She smiled her beautiful smile.

Everyone went home feeling good, feeling wonderful.

CHAPTER
7

Peanut's mother had made her costumes. One had a full red skirt that went right down to her ankles. With it she wore a white blouse trimmed with red at the neck and wrists and a black velvet vest. A velvet band held her hair in place. Her second costume, the one she would wear for the wedding, was a pink dress trimmed with ribbons and tiny flowers. She brought the costumes to school on hangers wrapped in cleaners' plastic.

"They're so pretty," Jilly sighed as she held

the door so Peanut wouldn't crush the costumes. "Pink is your best color. You're going
to be perfectly beautiful."

Peanut hoped — thought — she might be.
But it didn't seem proper to agree with Jilly.
Instead she said the thing she still felt. "The
only bad thing about this play is that you're
not in it. You look like a princess. You could
be the star."

Jilly — now that the play was so near, now
that she saw Peanut's costumes — almost
wished she had been brave enough to be in it.
Until she thought of standing up in front of
the whole school.

Peanut hung her costumes on the rack at
the back of the classroom as Jilly looked at
the others. The fuzzy animal costumes were
fun, even hanging limp. The prince costumes
were green and blue satin. King William the
Wonderful's costume was gold velvet. The
dragon costume wasn't there, though. Ollie
hadn't arrived yet.

Miss Kraft clapped her hands. "To your

seats, people. We still have the day to be got through before dress rehearsal. We'll start out by speaking the play aloud for a last review. Then we'll get on with our regular lessons. I fully expect you to learn — really learn — something today."

She looked around. "Ollie isn't here yet. Why does he choose today of all days to be late? Well, we'll get started without him. Jilly, suppose you take his part until he gets here."

Jilly had her copy of the play, but she didn't need it. After all the prompting practice, she knew every single line. So did everyone else. Even Elvis was letter perfect.

They had just reached the wedding when Mrs. Perrin, Mr. Granger's secretary, appeared at the door. Miss Kraft talked softly to her, then turned back to the class. A worried frown creased her forehead. "Can you take care of yourselves for just a little while? I have to see to something." She picked up a book off her desk and held it up. It was a mystery. "I plan on reading to you this afternoon — if you all behave today. Courtney, suppose you start reading aloud. I won't be gone long. Everybody be very quiet. I'm putting you on your honor."

She went out, closing the door behind her. Courtney stood up, faced the class, and opened the book. But nobody was ready to listen.

"What's going on?"

"Maybe Miss Maya had an accident."

"Maybe those wobbly trees fell down and smashed."

"You can't have a forest without trees."

"Listen, you guys," Courtney said above the hum. "We're on our honor. I'm going to start reading."

She did, and the whispering quieted.

She had almost finished the first chapter when Miss Kraft returned. "Oh good, you're doing what I asked. Thank you for being such great kids. Polly? Jilly? Please come with me."

What was happening?

Peanut and Jilly followed her to the gym.

Miss Maya was draped across one of the chairs in the first row, her hand over her eyes. She was the picture of despair.

"I asked you both to come because you're such good friends," Miss Kraft said to Peanut and Jilly. "You always back each other up."

Something bad was happening! Peanut and Jilly reached for each other's hands.

"Mrs. Burke called," said Miss Kraft. "Ollie has chicken pox."

The meaning of what she was saying flooded over Peanut and Jilly.

"But that means we can't have the play!" gasped Peanut.

"Everybody has worked so hard," moaned Jilly. "The kids will be so disappointed."

"A whole lot of people are going to be disappointed." Miss Maya spoke in a tragic voice. "The entire school is looking forward to tomorrow afternoon and the play."

Silence. Cold, heavy silence filled the gym, smothering all the memories of the last weeks' of laughter.

This couldn't be happening. Oh, it just

couldn't, not after all the excitement and fun and work of the past month.

"There is a possible way out of this problem," said Miss Kraft. "I'm going to make a suggestion and you can think about it. Jilly, you know Ollie's lines. You know how he's supposed to move around the stage. You know everything he's supposed to do. Would you consider taking his part?"

Oh, Miss Kraft must be joking!

Holding her breath, forgetting to breathe, Jilly searched Miss Kraft's face. No, she wasn't joking. She looked very serious.

How could she, Jilly, be Dragon Hotbreath? Oh, how could she? Why, she even found it hard to stand up in class — and she *knew* everybody in class. Tomorrow, all the kids at Alcott would be at the assembly. And Miss Kraft wanted her — her, Jillian Matthews — to jump around on the stage and roar and talk and — and — The idea was so awful that Jilly couldn't speak. Her mouth opened and closed, but not a word came out.

Miss Kraft studied Jilly's face. Then she hugged her close. "I wouldn't suggest this if I didn't think you could do it, honey. I want you to know that. You *can* do it — but you don't have to. If it's just too hard for you, I'll understand and so will Miss Maya. We give you our word we will never tell a soul we asked you. Just — think about it before you make up your mind one way or the other."

"But" — Jilly licked her lips — "if I'm the dragon, there won't be a stage manager and a prompter."

"I'll take your job as stage manager," said Miss Maya.

"I'll prompt," said Miss Kraft. "I won't let anybody miss a line."

"But . . . the dragon's a boy," Jilly protested. It was her last, strong argument.

"Who's to know that?" said Miss Maya. "Remember, he wears the dragon head."

A chill wind seemed to wrap itself around Jilly. Then a hot blast touched her. She became aware of Peanut's hand holding hers so hard it hurt and she was grateful that her best friend was with her.

"You need time to think," said Miss Kraft. "Suppose you and Polly talk this over. Why don't you go up on stage where you can be alone for a while."

Feeling as though she were a puppet made of sticks, Jilly followed Peanut across the gym . . . up the stairs . . . past dangling ropes and the unpainted backs of scenery trees . . . and out onto the stage. They sank down on the bench in front of the cottage.

"I'm going to die," Jilly wailed. "If I don't do it, everybody will be unhappy. If I do it, I might faint dead away. Or I might stand up there and not be able to say one single word. I might even throw up in front of everyone. Everybody will stare at me."

This was a nightmare. Pretty soon her mother would wake her up and say, "There, there. It's all just a bad dream."

But nobody awakened her.

"You know, there's a good part about being

Dragon Hotbreath," said Peanut.

Good? That's all Peanut knew!

"You'll be inside the dragon costume," Peanut went on. "Nobody will really be looking at you."

Oh! That was a new idea. "They'll look at the outside of what I'm inside of," Jilly said slowly, thoughtfully.

"Right," said Peanut. "And I'll be there with you all the time," she promised.

Jilly closed her eyes and imagined the awfulness of being onstage, of bounding around and roaring and everybody in the world staring at her.

"I know how shy you feel," Peanut said softly. "You know, being shy is a really nice part of you, Jilly. I like your shyness."

Jilly stared at her. Peanut was pulling her leg!

"I mean it," said Peanut. "You're quiet and gentle and it's all part of being shy the way you are."

A warm feeling flooded over Jilly.

"If you do this, Jilly," said Peanut, "it will be the bravest thing anybody in the whole world ever did."

Jilly sat there, Peanut beside her, facing up to things. She couldn't let everybody's fun be spoiled. She was the only one in the class who could do this. She was going to have to be Dragon Hotbreath.

"Okay," she said at last, her voice shaking. "I'll do it."

Peanut hugged her. "You are ab-so-lutely the bravest person I ever met. And I promise I'll stand close to you. If you faint — which you won't — I'll catch you. Who knows," she said, her brown eyes looking deep into Jilly's gray ones, "maybe you'll even have fun."

Fun? Fun! Ha!

So that is how gentle, shy Jilly turned into a dragon.

Mrs. Perrin volunteered to make another dragon costume in a hurry. Mr. Granger told her to take as much time as she needed — as long as she finished it in time for dress rehearsal.

66

Mr. Fortunato said he had an early model of the dragon head down in the arts and crafts room. "I can adapt it to fit Jilly," he said. "Maybe I'll put hinges on the jaws so she can open the dragon's mouth."

And Miss Maya practiced with Jilly for the rest of the morning. Jilly had to learn to dart in and out among the trees and pretend to breathe fire. She had to practice saying Hotbreath's lines in a loud voice.

"Speak to me way back here," Miss Maya called from the doorway of the gym. "Pretend you're putting your voice right onto my left shoulder."

Jilly tried. But, oh, it was so hard. . . .

That afternoon, at dress rehearsal, everyone looked at Jilly in awe. Imagine! She was taking a part in the play and she had never practiced. Imagine! Without her, there wouldn't even be a play. Why, she was a hero!

Jilly had something to learn at dress rehearsal, too. The dragon costume was finished, and she had to make the tail behave. It swung around behind her and bumped into things.

Backstage, between scenes, she pulled her arms out of the dragon sleeves, opened the dragon's jaws, and peeked out. If she had to be in the play, hers was surely the very best part. Nobody could see her!

And now that she was the dragon, she began to see things the way Ollie did. It was too bad that Hotbreath couldn't breathe fire. It would be lots more fun if, when Hotbreath opened his jaws and roared, fire came out of his mouth. . . .

Everyone had such a good time at dress rehearsal that they paid no attention to a fumble here and there. Like the gnomes saying their fifth act lines in the first act. Or the bears making the trees wobble when they stepped behind them so that the princes who were hiding there could take the bears' places. Or the golden flowers getting stuck and coming up only halfway when Mr. Fortunato pulled the ropes that were supposed to make them stand tall. Or the dragon who roared in a whisper.

"Good," Miss Maya called when the curtains closed. "I'm glad we had a few glitches. There's a saying in the theater — if dress rehearsal is perfect, the play will be full of things that go wrong. Our play is bound to be perfect."

Everyone grinned and hopped around and left the gym laughing and pushing. All except Jilly. Miss Maya still wanted a few minutes alone with her.

"All right, Dragon," Miss Maya called from the back of the gym. "Let's roar a little. I mean, a lot. I mean, make it LOUD."

Jilly tried. "Roar-rrrrr?"

"Oh, you can do better than that. Remember, your voice has to carry outside the dragon head. Make it like thunder."

Jilly opened Hotbreath's mouth wide on its hinges, took a long breath, and made her voice deep. "ROARRRRR!" she howled. "ROARRRRR!" It was the most glorious noise she had ever made. "ROARRRRR!"

"Wonderful," called Miss Maya, clapping.

Clapping came from among the trees and

Peanut stepped out. "Neat-o!" she yelled.

Jilly pulled off the dragon head. Her cheeks felt hot and she was grinning. It was fun to roar . . . not like Jillian Matthews . . . but like a dragon named Hotbreath.

CHAPTER 8

■▼■▼■▼■▼■▼■▼■▼■▼■▼■

The audience, tired of waiting, started chant-ing. "We want the play! We want the play! We want the play!"

It was the next afternoon. The classes had, as they usually did, come to the gym one at a time. Soon all the chairs were filled. It didn't take long for everybody to become restless and excited. This wasn't the regular kind of school assembly. They were going to see a play. This was something special.

Backstage, Miss Maya groaned. "Where are

our gnomes?" She looked around. "Boys," she called, "do not peek out through the curtains. Only amateurs peek. Don't you want to be real actors?"

Elvis and Nate turned away from the curtains as Gnome Elena came running, holding up her long beard so she wouldn't trip. "Miss Kraft said to tell you she'll be here in a minute. She's having trouble making Allison's beard stay stuck."

"Alexandra? Stephanie?" Miss Maya called. "Do you have your baskets?"

Peanut and Carrie held up the twig-filled baskets so she could see them.

"Dragon?" Miss Maya called, "Dragon Hotbreath — are you in place?"

Jilly withdrew her arms from the dragon costume's sleeves, and still inside the costume, opened the dragon's jaws wide so she could see out of the mask. "I'm here," she called, peeking from behind the trees.

Miss Maya flashed her beautiful smile at Jilly. "Break a leg, trooper."

Break a leg — that meant good luck in theater talk. Suddenly Jilly felt almost light-hearted, excited in the nicest way.

Yesterday's dress rehearsal had been the scariest thing she had ever done. But last night, thinking about it, she had to admit that it was a fun kind of scariness. There was a lot to be said for being . . . not Jilly Matthews . . . but somebody else.

It wasn't Jilly who roared; it was a dragon named Hotbreath.

It wasn't Jilly who had trouble with the dragon's long, swingy tail; it was Dragon Hotbreath whose tail bumped into things.

It wasn't Jilly talking; it was Dragon Hotbreath.

It was . . . like . . . she could do almost anything as Dragon Hotbreath — things she, Jilly Matthews, would never do.

Last night she had thought a lot about Ollie — poor chicken-poxy Ollie — wanting Dragon Hotbreath to breathe fire. Wouldn't it add a lot to the play if the audience could see the fire? It would be so much fun! She had come up with an idea about it. But — did she have the nerve to do it? She wasn't sure. She wasn't sure. . . .

One by one everybody in the cast found a reason for walking past Jilly. "Break a leg," they murmured. "Break a leg." "Break a leg." Even Elvis said it without giggling.

Only Peanut didn't say break a leg. "I'd hug you if I could, only you're so deep inside your costume I can't get near you." She laughed. "Hey, open up your mouth."

Jilly pried open Hotbreath's jaws. Peanut looked hard right into Jilly's eyes. "You," she said, speaking slowly, pausing between the words, "are .. going .. to .. be .. the .. best .. dragon .. that .. ever .. was. So there!" She turned and ran to her place, ready to make her entrance.

Jilly closed Hotbreath's mouth and became invisible once more, hidden inside the costume.

Gnome Allison raced onto the stage, her beard flying. "I'm here," she called. "I'm here."

She was followed closely by Miss Kraft with her script, ready to prompt anyone who forgot a line.

"To your places," called Miss Maya. "Quiet everyone. Curtain!"

Mr. Fortunato worked the ropes and the curtains parted.

The audience stopped talking. When the coughing and foot shuffling had died down, Miss Maya said, "Now, Kevin," and gave him a gentle push.

Kevin stepped out in front of the cottage, holding up a card that was nearly as tall as he was. *Act I* was lettered on the card. "Act one," he said loudly and read from the back of the card, "Once upon a time there was a poor widow who lived in a forest with her two beautiful daughters. . . . "

Peanut-Stephanie and Carrie-Alexandra stepped onto the stage. Peanut looked down. "Oh, oh, dear sister. Look at this nice piece of dry wood right here near our very own cottage."

"Why, thank you, dear Stephanie," said

Carrie, adding it to the twigs in her basket. "I almost stumbled over it."

Jilly got ready. It was nearly time to make her entrance.

Mother-Courtney came out of the cottage with a big bowl of porridge. She set it on the table in front of the door. "There is just enough for the three of us," she said.

"Our food is nearly gone," sighed Alexandra.

"Whatever will we eat tomorrow?" said Stephanie.

There! That was Jilly's cue.

Letting out a roar that wasn't much more than a squeak, she leaped into view, forgetting Dragon Hotbreath's tail. Behind her, it banged into a tree. The tree swayed. It rocked slowwwly — the audience gasped — from siiide to siiide. It rocked for what seemed like a thousand years. Then it settled back into place. The audience breathed a sigh of relief.

Jilly tried the roar again. "Ruhhhhr." That was better. It had to be a roar, because that's what dragons do. But it wasn't meant to scare the poor widow and her daughters. "I have not eaten in six months," Jilly said, making her voice pitiful. "I am weak."

There was silence in the gym.

"Dear ladies," Jilly said in her best, deep, dragon-sounding voice, "will you share your porridge with a poor, starving dragon?"

Well, of course Stephanie and Alexandra and their mother — who could see beauty and goodness in this dragon — agreed. They didn't know he was King William the Wonderful or, as the play went on, that the bears who came to join him were really his sons, placed under an enchantment by the wicked gnomes who had stolen the king's gold and changed it into a field of droopy flowers.

Between acts, the audience was noisy, calling and whistling shrilly. But silence returned to the gym each time the curtains parted and Kevin announced another act.

They had almost reached the part where Dragon Hotbreath was going to come to Stephanie and Alexandra's rescue. Jilly was still undecided about her idea. Should she? Should she not? Maybe she should have talked things over with Miss Maya. But Miss Maya had been so busy today, with so many things on her mind. . . .

Stephanie and Alexandra huddled against the rock wall outside the gnomes' cave. They had stumbled into this place without knowing that it was the gnomes' hideaway. The gnomes were hopping up and down in front of them.

"Silly geese," cackled Gnome Allison, "you should have known better than to wander around the forest just to pick up wood."

"But we need wood for our fire," Stephanie said bravely. "And we are not afraid of you, funny little man." But she shook while she said that. The audience could see that she was shivering.

"Funny little man indeed!" screeched Gnome Elena.

"For that you must be put under a spell," shrieked Gnome Allison. She stamped her foot, catching her long beard. It started to pull away from her chin. She grabbed it and held it in place.

"Please, not a spell," moaned Stephanie.

"Please, sirs." She and Alexandra clutched at each other.

"You," growled Allison, her hand to her chin, looking as though she had a toothache, "shall become a pair of frogs. Frogs you will be until the day you — "

"Enough, you horrible gnomes!" yelled Jilly, hopping out from among the rocks as fast as she could, considering her tail. "You shall not harm these lovely girls. I will blast you away with my fiery breath."

"Neither fire nor flea can hurt me," howled Elena.

"Silly dragon," laughed Allison, "you can't hurt us. You are our made-up creature."

"Says you!" roared Dragon Hotbreath. Jilly had made up her mind. She opened Hotbreath's jaws, took a deep breath, and began blowing out the long red banana balloon she had kept in her pocket since last night. Out, out, out the red balloon reached with each breath.

Allison and Elena stood staring. What was happening? They had not practiced this. Dragon Hotbreath was supposed to chase them offstage

where nobody could see him turning them into cinders.

The audience howled. "Let 'em have it, Hotbreath! Let 'em have it!"

Jilly forced a final puff of air into the balloon. It became immensely long before, with a resounding POW!, it exploded.

Allison and Elena turned and ran offstage, Jilly hot on their heels.

The audience yelled and clapped and stamped their feet.

Backstage, Miss Maya and Miss Kraft stood with their arms around each other, their heads resting on each other's shoulders, shaking. Were they sobbing? Were Miss Maya and Miss Kraft crying?

The audience had trouble settling back down after the big dragon blast. They didn't pay as much attention as they should to Hotbreath gently watering the wilted flowers. Jilly had to pay attention, though. She had to be careful to tilt the sprinkling can only over the places where pans could catch the water, or the stage would be flooded out.

The audience did quiet down and pay attention when the flowers, with Mr. Fortunato's help, began to rise in golden splendor. "Awwwww," they crooned. "Awwwww."

Jilly sank down and stretched out flat on her stomach, hoping Hotbreath's tail wasn't sticking up above the flowers.

"Now, King William, now," Miss Maya called softly from offstage.

Straightening his crown, David stood up. "At last," he said. "At last I am free of the gnomes' wicked enchantment."

The audience clapped, and they clapped again when the bears stepped behind the trees and Prince Bryan and Prince Ryan emerged.

The wedding of King William the Wonderful and the girls' mother was beautiful. Stephanie and Alexandra wore matching pink dresses and carried golden flowers, and Prince Bryan and Prince Ryan wore crowns of golden flowers. The gym was quiet to the very end of the play, when Kevin stepped out with a card that read *The End* and recited, without even reading, "And they all lived happily ever after."

A satisfied breath gusted through the gym. It was followed by thunderous applause.

The actors came back onstage, the whole string of them, holding hands.

The clapping got louder and the boys whistled and stomped their feet.

The actors bowed, as Miss Maya had taught them.

"Authors!" A voice boomed out over the applause. It was Mr. Granger. "Authors! Hear, hear!"

Backstage, Jilly and Peanut stared at each other. What were they supposed to do?

Miss Kraft hugged them — which was quite hard to do, with Jilly still inside her costume. "Mr. Granger wants you to take a bow by yourselves."

Peanut started to go back onstage, dragging Jilly after her.

"Wait," said Miss Kraft. "Jilly, it was fine to take your curtain call wearing Hotbreath's costume. But don't you think you might take off the dragon head and be Jilly Matthews? Dragon Hotbreath didn't write this play. Polly and Jilly did."

"Authors!" came the call from the audience. Now the kids were yelling it, too. "Authors!"

Inside her comfortable costume, Jilly thought about what Miss Kraft had just said.

"Aw, come on, Jill," pleaded Peanut. "You can do it."

Jilly reached up and took off the dragon head. Then, carrying it with her, she followed Peanut onstage. She was Jillian Matthews. And she faced all those people. But she could not have done it if her best friend, Peanut, hadn't been holding her hand.

Look for #6

Peanut in Charge

Peanut bounded up the steps two at a time, Jilly close behind her. At the top of the stairs she stopped dead, staring at the carpeting outside the bathroom. It was covered with small, white footprints. She tiptoed to the door and looked in.

The two halves of a baby powder box lay upside down beside the tub. Powder covered the pink tile floor. The twins — powdery white from their curls to their toes — knelt in the middle of the mess, patting it, stirring it, having a perfectly lovely time.

"Inside snow," Bridget explained, looking up at Peanut.

"We're making snowballs," said Deirdre.

They flung handfuls of it into the air.

Peanut and Jilly turned sick smiles on each other. Never in the whole history of Evanston, in the whole history of baby-sitting, had there been such a mess.

Fun is just around the corner...

39 Kids on the Block™

by Jean Marzollo

When you live on the same block with these 39 kids, you're sure to find mischief, adventure, and lots of surprises! Meet them all in this terrific new series!

Great New Series!